© 1994 Geddes & Grosset Ltd
Published by Geddes & Grosset Ltd,
New Lanark, Scotland.

ISBN 1 85534 568 4

Printed and bound in Slovenia.

The Pied Piper of Hamelin

Retold by Judy Hamilton
Illustrated by Lindsay Duff

Tarantula Books

The town of Hamelin was a prosperous town and the people of Hamelin were contented and proud to live there. And then the rats came.

There are rats in every town and they can be a nuisance sometimes, but usually they can be kept under control. But when the rats came to Hamelin town, they came in their thousands. Nobody had ever seen so many rats in one place. They swarmed all over the city, stealing food, gnawing their way into buildings everywhere, spreading germs and disease. The rat-catchers worked day and night to try to rid the city of the rats but it seemed that the more rats they killed, the more rats appeared to take their places.

The people of the town were miserable.

Things got worse as time went on. The rats were eating their way through every larder in the town, every warehouse and foodstore. Everywhere they went, they left mess and destruction. Food was becoming scarce and people were afraid of going hungry. Children and old people were falling sick from eating food which the rats had contaminated.

In desperation, the mayor of the town called a meeting to see if anything could be done to get rid of the plague of rats. Everyone gathered in the town square. Every time an idea was mentioned, someone else would say that it had already been tried and had failed.

Then a stranger stepped in front of the crowd.

The stranger was dressed in very unusual and brightly-coloured clothes, and on his head he wore a large hat with a peacock's feather in it. He looked as if he would feel more at home in a circus. All the people of Hamelin stared at him as he began to speak in a strange, sing-song voice:

"If you want the rats to leave this city, then I can help you, but make no mistake, it will cost you dearly," he said.

"This city has ten thousand pieces of gold in its treasuries," said the mayor. "If you can rid this city of the plague of rats, then the gold shall all be yours. But tell us first, good sir, how do you propose to work this miracle?"

The stranger smiled secretively.

"I have all that I need right here, tucked in my belt," he said, pointing to a wooden pipe at his waist. "If you want me to get rid of the rats, then you must trust me to do it my way."

The mayor was not very sure that the stranger could do as he said, but he could see no harm in letting him try, so he agreed. The piper then turned towards the crowd.

"You can all go back to your homes now, and wait until I have completed my task," he said.

Everyone left the town square and went home, wondering what the stranger in bright clothing would do.

Once everyone was out of the way, the stranger took out his pipe and began to play. The haunting melody which he played filtered through the town. As if by magic, the people saw the rats leaving their houses one after another in procession. They looked out of their windows to see thousand upon thousand of the rats hurrying together towards the town square where the piper was playing. As the first rats drew near to him, the piper began to dance and turned to move off down the street that led out of the town, with the rats following behind. The procession of rats grew and grew to astonishing proportions. Every single one of them appeared to follow the sound of the music as the piper danced on.

The people watched in amazement as the piper danced on out of sight. Some people, unable to contain their curiosity, came out of their houses and followed the enormous procession of rats. The piper danced on without looking back until he came to the bridge which crossed the river at the edge of the town. When he reached the bridge, he stopped dancing but continued to play. The people who had followed then saw the rats run to the edge of the fast-flowing river. One by one, the rats began to jump off the riverbank and into the river, where the current carried them off and out of sight. One after another, thousands and thousands of rats jumped into the river and disappeared, until every single one had gone.

The townspeople could not believe what had just happened. When they returned to their home and shops, no matter how hard they looked, they could find no rats. They called another meeting i the town square. The piper had to be given his reward.

However, the townspeople did not know that the mayor had been lying when he had told the piper that there were ten thousand pieces of gold in the treasury. The mayor was a foolish and greedy man and had spent much of the town's money on himself. The treasury was nearly empty. When the piper came to collect his reward, it was only to find that the mayor could pay him no more than a few coins for his trouble

The piper was very angry. He blamed the whole town for the mayor's deceit.

"You have all tricked me and humiliated me!" he cried in rage. "But let me tell you this; nobody treats the Pied Piper in this way without suffering for it! You shall all be punished!"

With these words, the Pied Piper turned from the crowd and took out his pipe once again. Putting it to his lips, he began to play, but this time he played a different tune. The music reached every corner of the town and set the feet of every child in Hamelin dancing. The grown-ups watched in horror as all the children formed a procession, just as the rats had done, and began to follow the Pied Piper.

Fathers and mothers called out to their children to stop, but the children did not seem to hear. Faster and faster they danced after the Pied Piper. The townspeople could do nothing to stop them. On and on the Piper danced and the children followed happily behind. The music had a magical quality, which only they could hear, but it made them want to go on and on.

Just as before, the Pied Piper led the procession along the road which led out of town. The townspeople watched in horror as he approached the bridge over the river, but the children did not jump into the water as the rats had done. They followed the Pied Piper right over the bridge and on into the distance.

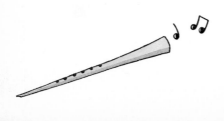

At the end of the procession, lagging behind the others because he could not go so fast, was a little boy with a weak leg. He found walking quite a struggle and got very tired. But even he was happy to go wherever the magical music led him and although he could not go as fast as the others he did his very best to keep up. Something told him that the children were being taken to a place more wonderful than anything they could possibly imagine.

The townspeople stopped. Somehow, they knew that the Pied Piper had taken their children for ever and that they would never be able to get them back. They turned sadly for home.

The town of Hamelin was plunged into deep mourning from that day onwards. A town without any children is a very sad place. The parents of the children were heartbroken and every grown-up knew and loved some of the children who had gone. The mayor, having realised what his wickedness had done, left the town in shame.

The townspeople did not know where their children had gone, not even whether they were alive or dead.

And then, some weeks later, the little boy with the weak leg limped back into Hamelin one day, exhausted and full of despair, with a strange tale to tell.

The Pied Piper had led the children for miles over the hills, with the sound of his playing. The little boy had tried to keep up, but as time went on, he fell farther behind. The Piper had led the children to the side of a steep mountain. The mountainside had opened up and in the distance could be seen the most beautiful place. The children passed through the mountain one by one but just as the little lame boy had reached the opening, it had closed up. He had been left alone by the mountain, desolate because he could not go with his friends.

The town had paid dearly for getting rid of the rats. It was eerie and quiet without the sound of playing children for many years to come.